D1031522

AN UGLYDOLL COMIC

EAT DAT!

WITHDRAWN

KIM | HORVATH | NICHOLS | JACOBSON | MCGINTY | COOPER | LEDBETTER

EAT DAT!

AN UGLYDOLL COMIC

COVER ART: SUN-MIN KIM AND DAVID HORVATH
COVER AND BOOK DESIGN: FAWN LAU
EDITOR: TRACI N. TODD

TM, ® and © 2013, Pretty Ugly, LLC. All Rights Reserved.

The stories, characters and incidents mentioned in this publication are entirely fictional.

No portion of this book may be reproduced without written permission from the copyright holders.

Printed in China

Published by VIZ Media, LLC
P.O. Box 77010
San Francisco, CA 94107

10 9 8 7 6 5 4 3 2 1
First printing, January 2014

End papers by Sun-Min Kim and David Horvath | **"Food Fight"** story by Travis Nichols, art by Ian McGinty, colors by Michael E. Wiggam | **"No Share"** part 1 story and art by Sun-Min Kim and David Horvath | **"Taste Buds"** story by Travis Nichols, art by Phillip Jacobson, colors by Michael E. Wiggam | **"Samplin'"** story by Travis Nichols, art by Ian McGinty, colors by Michael E. Wiggam | **"Treeberry Pie"** story and art by Dave Cooper | **"Flavorville"** story by Travis Nichols, art by Phillip Jacobson, colors by Michael E. Wiggam | **"No Share"** part 2 story and art by Sun-Min Kim and David Horvath | **"Babo's Bakery"** story by Travis Nichols, art by Ian McGinty, colors by Michael E. Wiggam | **"Delicious"** story and art by Joe Ledbetter | **"Mover and Little Bent's Lunch on the Gooooo"** story and art by Travis Nichols | **"Don't Overdo It"** story and art by Sun-Min Kim and David Horvath | **"Hot in the Shade"** story by Travis Nichols, art by Phillip Jacobson, colors by Michael E. Wiggam | **"Sweet Victory"** story by Travis Nichols, art by Phillip Jacobson, colors by Michael E. Wiggam | **"Black Belt Juice Ninjanator"** story and art by Travis Nichols | **"Stone Soup"** story by Travis Nichols, art by Ian McGinty, colors by Michael E. Wiggam | **"Back in the Ugly Day"** story and art by Sun-Min Kim and David Horvath

TABLE OF CONTENTS

Who Dat? — 6
Food Fight! — 9
No Share part 1 — 17
Taste Buds — 18
Samplin' — 24
Treeberry Pie — 31
Flavorville — 35
No Share part 2 — 41
Babo's Bakery — 42
Delicious — 52
Mover and Little Bent's Lunch on the Gooooo — 55
Don't Overdo It — 57
Hot in the Shade — 58
Sweet Victory — 64
Black Belt Juice Ninjanator — 68
Stone Soup — 73
Back in the Ugly Day — 77
Brought to You By — 78

WHO
BABO
WEDGEHEAD
NINJA
BATTY
SHOGUN
MYNUS
ICE-BAT

DAT?
BIG TOE
TRAY
OX
JEERO
WAGE
CANDY

FOOD FiGHT!
HELLO! WELCOME TO... FOOD COMPETITION SHOW!
We're... still working on the name. Heh.
UGLY 2 TV
TODAY'S BATTLE IS BETWEEN TWO CULINARY SORCERERS...
TRAY! AND SOFTY!
TRAY IS THE GENIUS BEHIND SUCH WONDERS AS FLYING A ROCKET TO THE MOON AND TURNING GOLD INTO SUGAR!
TRAY, HOW ARE YOU FEELING?
FEELING CONFIDENT, BIG TOE.

SOFTY! YOU'VE RECENTLY MASTERED COUNTING TO SIX!
WELL, I DON'T KNOW ABOUT *MASTERED*, BIG TOE!
ALRIGHTY THEN. LET'S DO THIS! *TO YOUR STATIONS!*
THREE... TWO...ONE... *MAKE FOOD!*
I'M PREPARING A FEAST FOR ALL *EIGHT* SENSES. IT'S ONE PART CHEMISTRY, ONE PART GASTRONOMY AND ONE PART ASTROLOGY. SHIELD YOUR EYES.
FWOOOSH!

HOW EXCITING TO SEE SCIENCE IN THE KITCHEN!
SOFTY... WHAT'RE YOU UP TO OVER HERE?
GLY 2 TV
CORN
CRACK!
I'M MAKING MY SPECIAL BREAK-AND-TEAR SALAD.
I...I'M NOT ALLOWED TO USE KNIVES. Or ovens.
RIP!
I WISH WE'D HAD THAT INFORMATION EARLIER.
WELL...MAY THE BEST UGLY WIN!

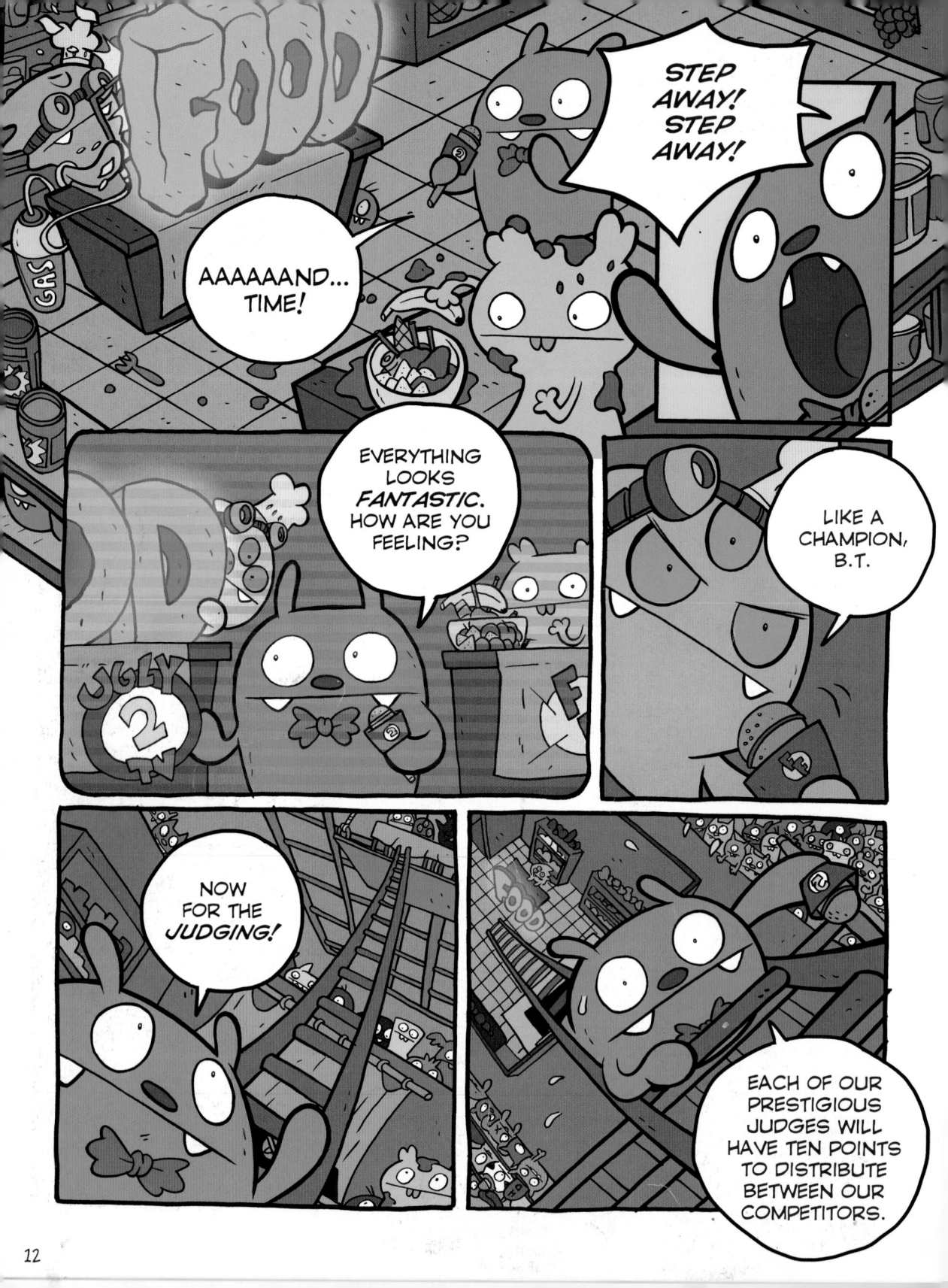
STEP AWAY! STEP AWAY!
AAAAAAND... TIME!
EVERYTHING LOOKS *FANTASTIC*. HOW ARE YOU FEELING?
LIKE A CHAMPION, B.T.
NOW FOR THE *JUDGING!*
EACH OF OUR PRESTIGIOUS JUDGES WILL HAVE TEN POINTS TO DISTRIBUTE BETWEEN OUR COMPETITORS.

WHEW! THIS TABLE IS WAY TOO HIGH. I MEAN... GASP! I GET WANTING TO BE DRAMATIC, BUT STILL.
OKAY! TO OUR JUDGES!
HE'S GHOSTY! TAKE IT AWAY, GHOST-AAAY!
UGLY 2 TV
CHEW CHEW CHEW!
GULP
MMHMM. MMHMM...
!
PLOP!
PLUP!
WAAA! DON'T LOOK AT ME! DON'T LOOK AT ME!
YUM SHOW
UTV

Should we just keep going? I don't... OKAY! JUDGE NUMBER TWO!
HE'S FRIENDLY! HE'S AN OVER-ACHIEVER! HE'S A VISION IN A BLUE APRON!
UGLY 2 TV
HE'S WAGE! LET'S HEAR IT!
THEY'RE BOTH WONDERFUL. SUCH GOOD FRIENDS.
I GIVE FIVE POINTS TO TRAY...
...AND FIVE POINTS TO SOFTY!
WE HAVE A TIE! A TIE!

EVERYTHING HINGES ON THE DECISION OF OUR THIRD AND FINAL JUDGE.
UGLY 2 TV
HE'S LIVELY! HE'S WILD! HE'S... A BIT OF A TROUBLE-MAKER!
HE'S GASSY! (AND HE HASN'T EVEN TRIED THE FOOD...)
Very funny. WELL, BIG T. TASTE ISN'T EVERYTHING. THE REAL TEST IS HOW WELL THIS STICKS TO THE WALL!
BOOM SHAKA LAKA!
SMASH!
PING
[INSERT NAME OF SHOW HERE] CHAMPION

OOPS.
NO NO NO NO NO NO NO NO NO NO!
WELL, I GUESS THAT'S THE END OF OUR SHOW... RIGHT AFTER WE DECLARE...
THE WINNERS!!
THE END

NO SHARE PART 1
YOU NEVER SHARE.
WHAT DAT.
MAY I TRY?
PEACE OUT.
OH, MAY I?
NOT FOR RENT.
BREAK ME OFF A LITTLE?
CAN'T TOUCH THIS.
LEMME STEAL A BITE...
HELP. POLICE.
HAVE YOU EVER SHARED A COOKIE?
There was that one time.
WANT SOME?
To be continued...

TASTE BUDS
THE NOGGIN SCRAMBLER BOASTS THE LARGEST LOOP- DE-LOOP IN ROLLER-COASTER HISTORY!
OOH. LOOPS.
CRUNCH
HEY, THIS IS PRETTY GOOD!
CRUNCH CRUNCH
INDEED. JUST A HINT OF SEA SALT TO COUNTER THE FRUITY SWEETNESS OF WILD BLUEBERRY AND CANE JUICE.
CLICK
HUH?

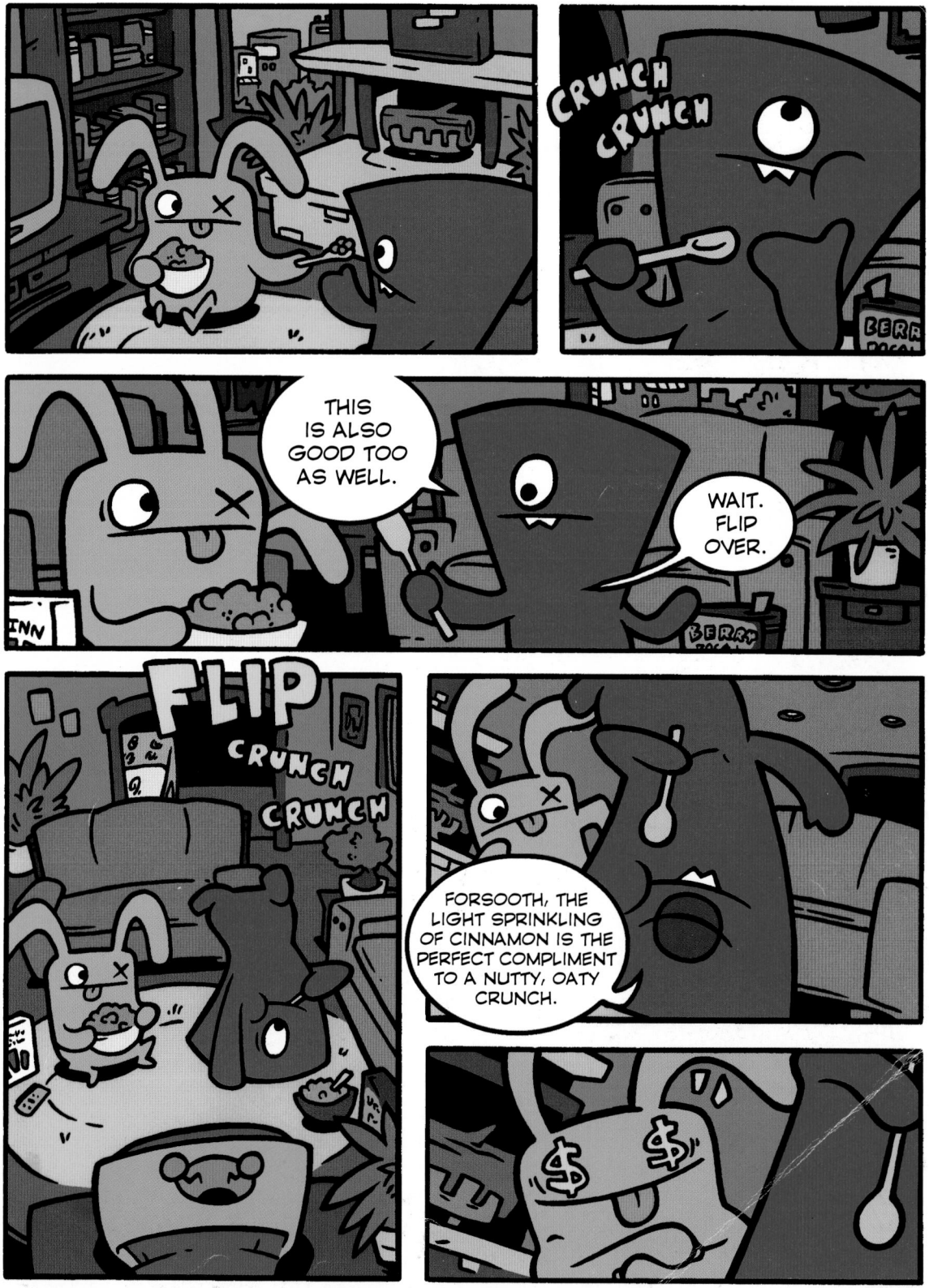
CRUNCH CRUNCH
THIS IS ALSO GOOD TOO AS WELL.
WAIT. FLIP OVER.
FLIP
CRUNCH CRUNCH
FORSOOTH, THE LIGHT SPRINKLING OF CINNAMON IS THE PERFECT COMPLIMENT TO A NUTTY, OATY CRUNCH.

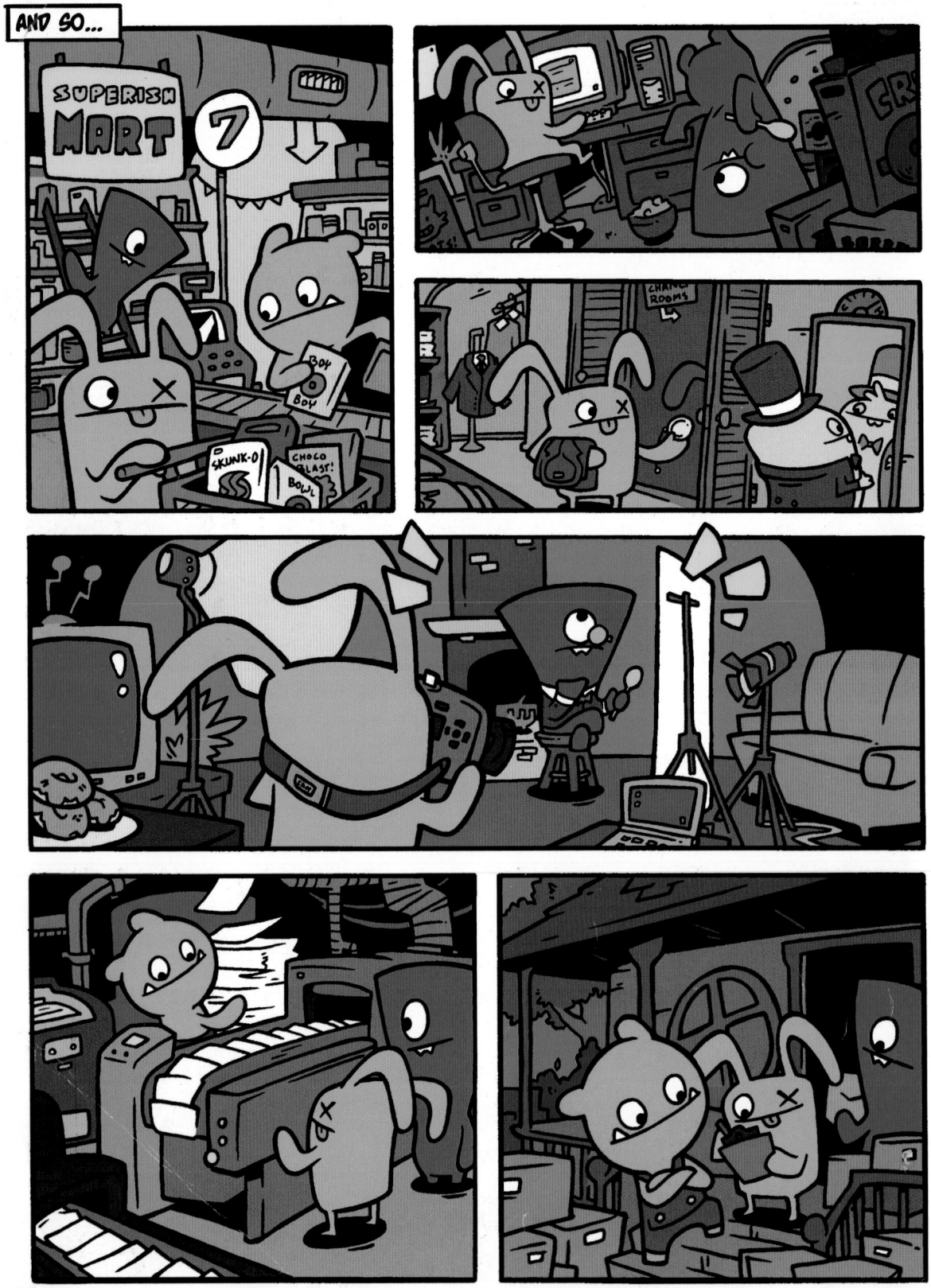
AND SO...
SUPERISH MART
7
BOY BOY
SKUNK-O
CHOCO BLAST!
BOWL
CHANGE ROOMS

UNTIL FINALLY...
UPSIDE DOWNLICIOUS
CULINARY COMMENTARY BY WEDGINALD J. HEAD
THIS IS IT, WEDGINALD. WE'RE GONNA BE WICH!
WHAT?
SALE?
SALE?
HMMM... "THE MINGLING OF COCOA AND VANILLA TAKES ONE ON A PLEASANT VOYAGE TO THE SOURCE OF ALL.
"THE PUFFED CORN IS THE SHIP, AND ON A SEA OF WHIMSY WE GO. TOGETHER."

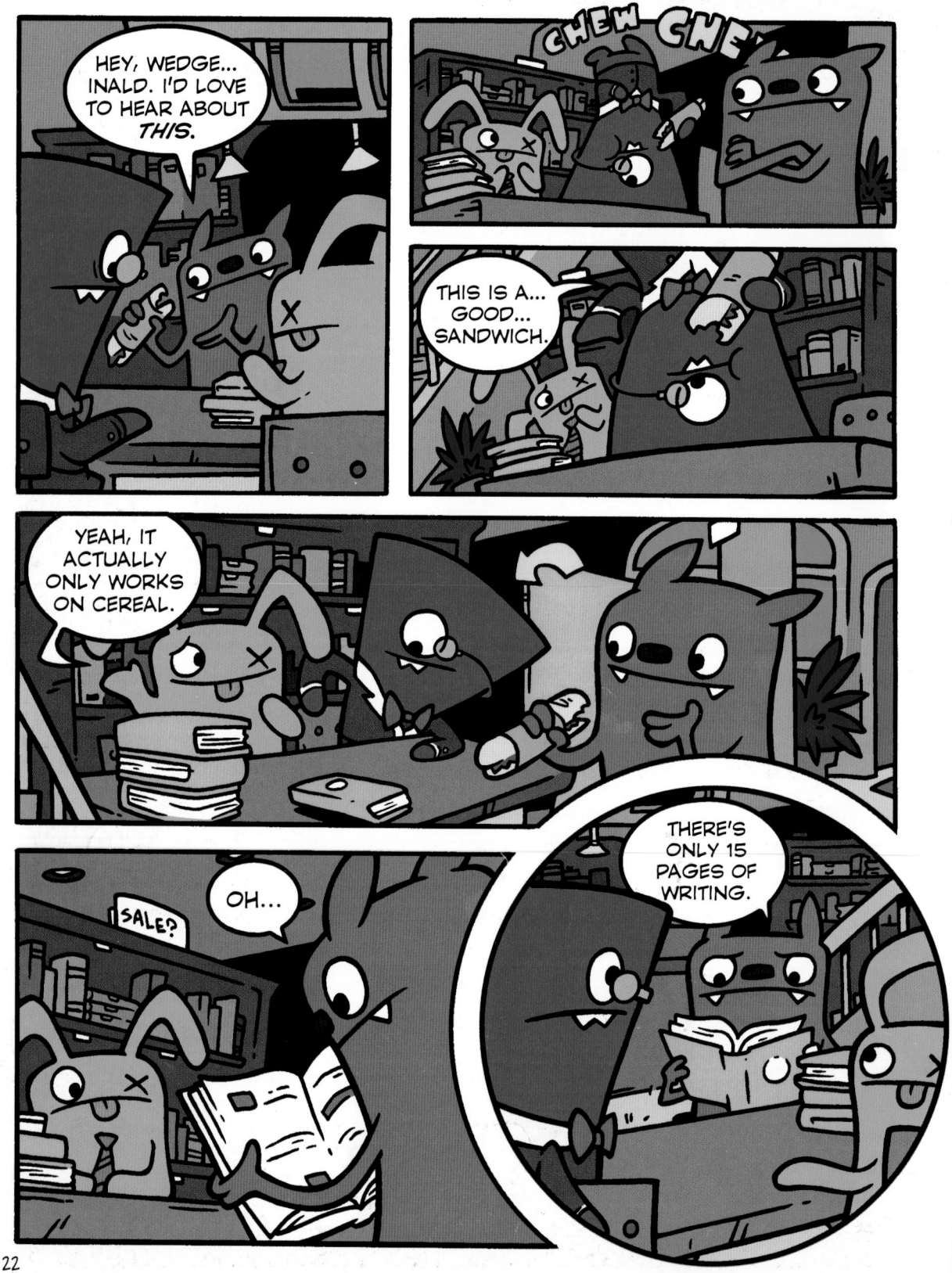
HEY, WEDGE... INALD. I'D LOVE TO HEAR ABOUT *THIS*.
CHEW CHE
THIS IS A... GOOD... SANDWICH.
YEAH, IT ACTUALLY ONLY WORKS ON CEREAL.
SALE?
OH...
THERE'S ONLY 15 PAGES OF WRITING.

AND THERE'S THIS BIG HOLE IN THE REST.
OH! THAT, YOU LUCKY DUCK, IS A BUILT-IN CEREAL BOWL!
2%
THAT...IS AMAZING.
SIR, I'M GOING TO HAVE TO ASK YOU TO PAY FOR THAT.
YIKES!
GUESS AGAIN.
EACH BITE, A POEM RECITED IN A WHISPER. A VERSE OF FIVE FRUITY SHAPES DELIVERED STRAIGHT TO MY SOUL...
END!

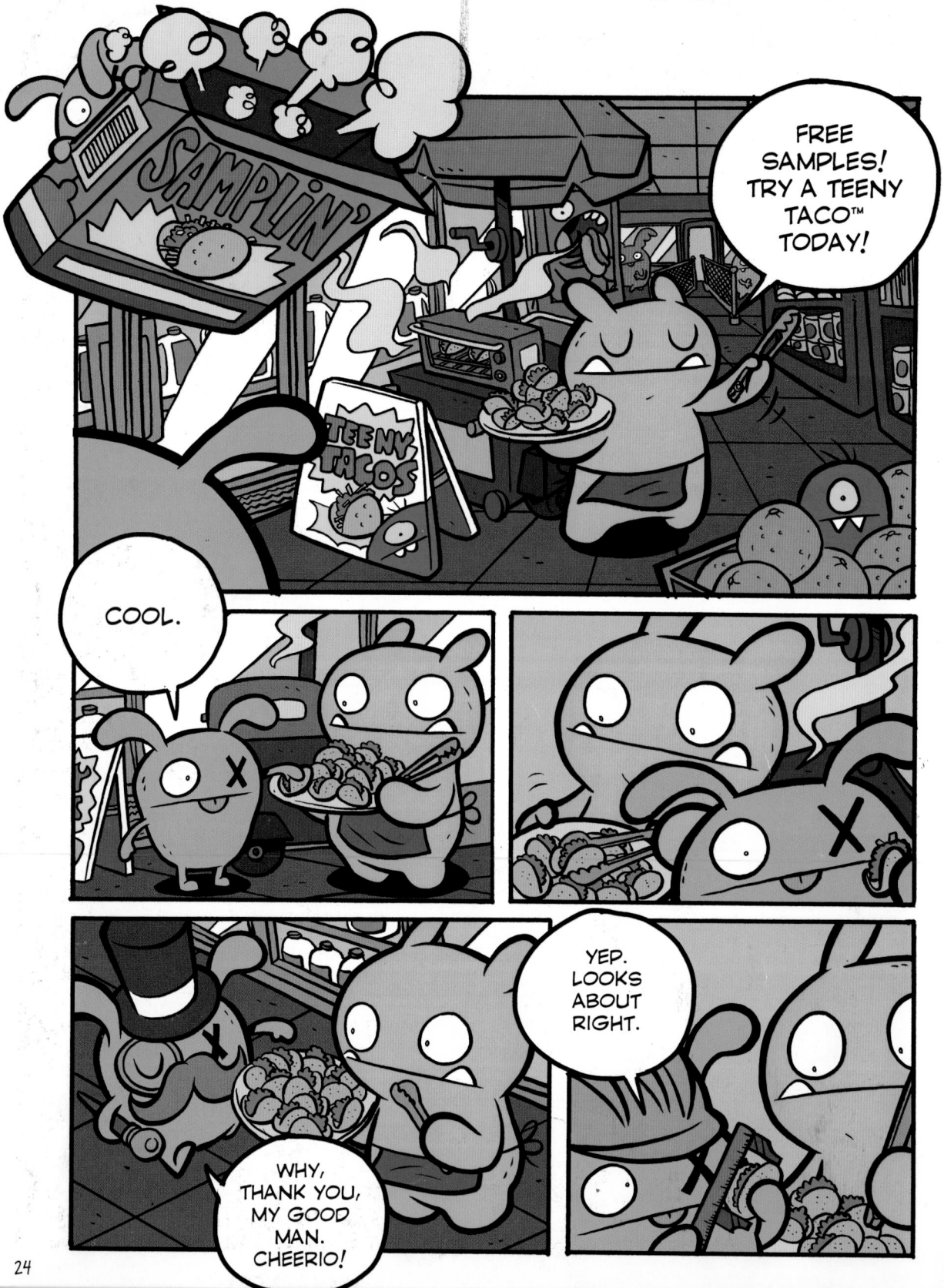
SAMPLIN'
TEENY TACOS
FREE SAMPLES! TRY A TEENY TACO™ TODAY!
COOL.
YEP. LOOKS ABOUT RIGHT.
WHY, THANK YOU, MY GOOD MAN. CHEERIO!

WELL, SHUCKS! LIL' OL' TACOS!
MUCH OBLIGED, TENDERFOOT.
TRICK OR TACO!
YAR! TACO OFF THE STARBOARD BOW!
HELLO. I AM WEDGEHEAD.
WHOOOOOOA! GNARLY TACOS, BRAH!

Shuffle Shuffle
NAB!
WHAT YEAR IS IT? ARE THERE STILL TACOS? *ARE THERE?*
YOU HAVE JUST SAVED THE GALAXY!
GOO-GOO GAH-GAH! ME WANT TACO!
WOOD!
CLOMP CLOMP CLOMP!

SIGH.
MAS
NO MÁS
PSST!
YOU ARE INVITED
(flip over)
STORE
WAGE
YOU ARE
(flip over)

FROZEN FOOD
2
3
OKIES
$2
FRO ZEN SOCKS
JUST SAUSAGES!
A TON O' BEAN

FLOWERS

FAKE FLOWERS
NOT REAL!

IRREGULAR
NO GOOD
MAYBE
SPORT
SPORTS
SMALL
BIG

BASEBALL CARDS
JELLY
CHIPS
BOOKS
PEAS
BIKE TIRES
BABY BIRDS
PILES OF STUFF
SAND
HOME GOODS
RUITS
OUTDOOR FURNITURE
WELCOME!

DINNER IS SERVED!
I...I DON'T KNOW WHAT TO SAY, OX. THANK YOU!
I'M SO HAPPY YOU LIKED IT. AND NOW, YOUR BILL.
WILL THAT BE CASH OR CHARGE?
PLOP!
end!

TREEBERRY PIE
2013
with colour assistance by Jill Wisniowski
RING RING!
ZZZZZZ
ROLL
ZZZ
TOWER!
TEETER
GROW
?
GROWL
!

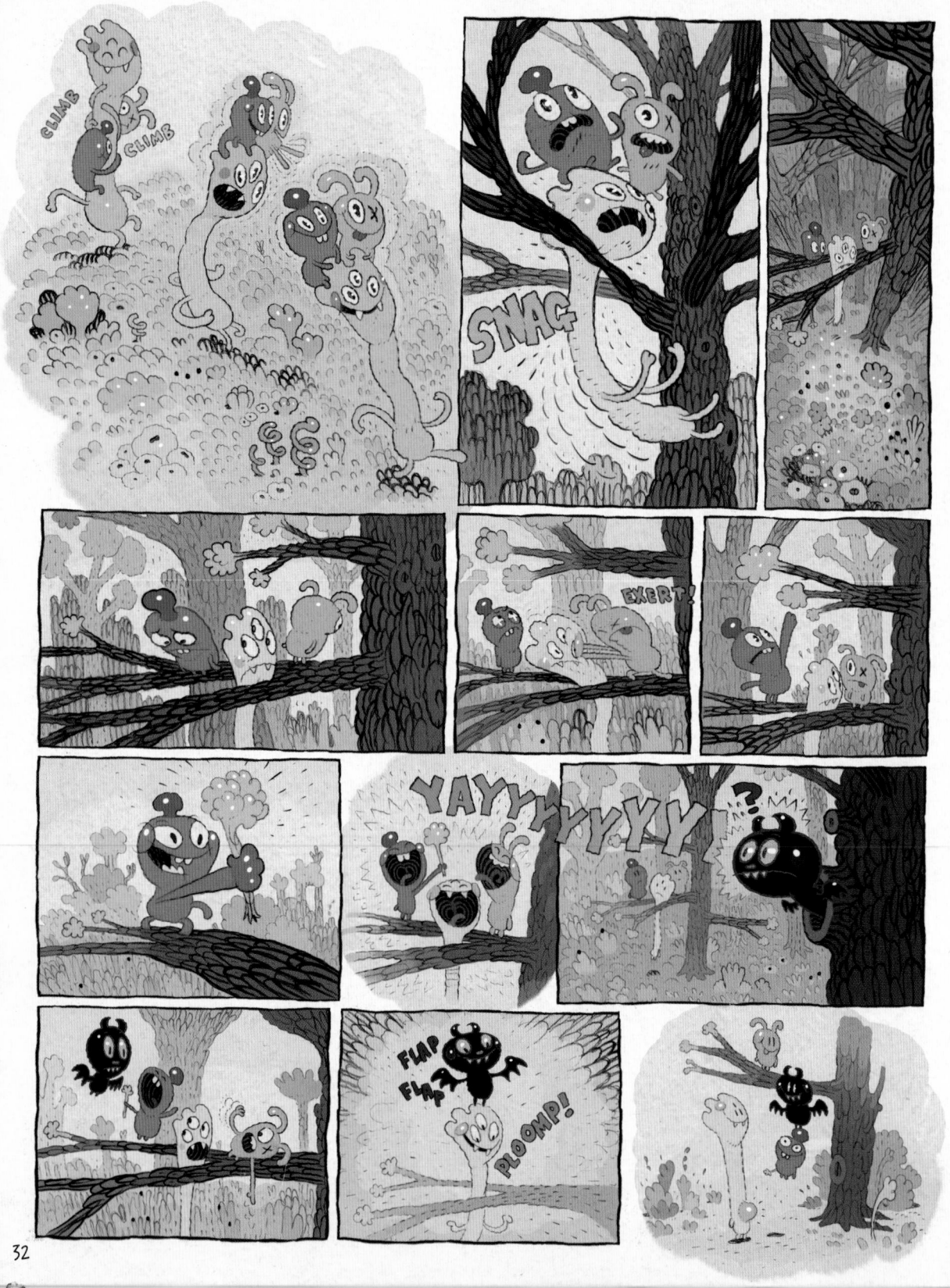
CLIMB
CLIMB
SNAG
EXERT!
YAYYYYYYYY
?
FLAP
FLAP
PLOOMP!

GRUMBLE
GURGLE
BURRPPPPP
THROW
THUD
WIND
WIND
TICK TICK
TICK
THE BEGINNING

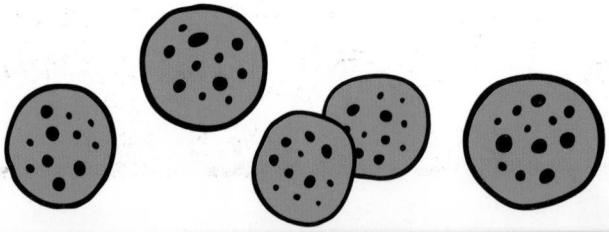

FLAVOR VILLE
HEY EVERYONE! TRAY'S BACK!

HOW WAS YOUR TRIP?

IT WAS *GREAT*. I BROUGHT BACK SOMETHING REALLY COOL.

THEY'RE CALLED WÄCKŸ FRÜTS.
THEY FOOL WITH YOUR TONGUE. MAKE THINGS TASTE DIFFERENT.

CHEW CHEW CHEW

MY TONGUE IS TINGLING.
COOK

WHOA!

YOURS TOO, ICE-BAT!

OKAY! LET'S EAT!

IT TASTES LIKE A TELEPHONE POLE!
TASTES LIKE A HUBCAP!

DO-NUT
CALL 6522S
LOST
CALL 5225L
FOUND
HERE GOES...

ENCHI-LADAS!
FOUND
WHAT THE?!

CINNAMON TOAST!

EGG-ROLLS! NICE!

SALT-WATER TAFFY? WOW!

WOO! CAREFUL, GUYS. THIS WINDOW IS SPICY.

OOH! GUACAMOLE!
BIG BOY

OOH! THAT'D GO GREAT WITH THESE TORTILLA CHIPS!

TRAY! OVER HERE!
BLUE-BERRY PIE!
YOU'RE WELCOME.

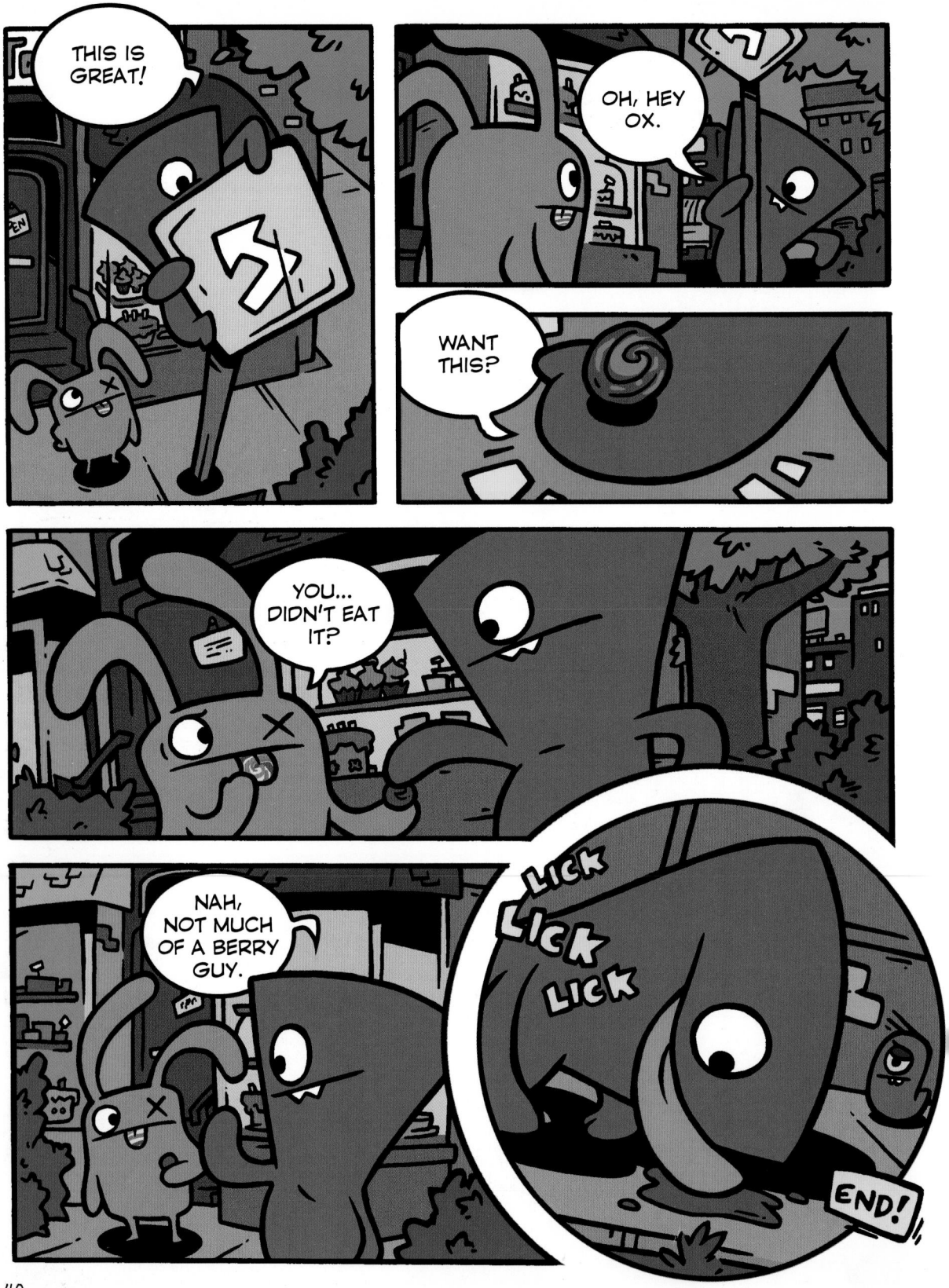
THIS IS GREAT!
OH, HEY OX.
WANT THIS?
YOU... DIDN'T EAT IT?
NAH, NOT MUCH OF A BERRY GUY.
LICK LICK LICK
END!

NO SHARE PART 2
SO WHY DON'T YOU SHARE, MAN?
WHAT DAT.
WHAT YOU NEED IS A COOKIE STUNT DOUBLE.
FROM NOW ON... BUY TWO COOKIES.
Cookie Bake #2
SO NOW WHEN YOU ARE ASKED TO SHARE... YOU HAVE AN EXTRA ONE.
STUNT DOUBLE.
THAT'S MESSED UP.

BABO'S bakery
BACK
BUTTER COOKIES
CHOC.CHIP COOKIES
hi
BOOM BOX
TWO CHOCOLATE CHIP COOKIES, PLEASE.
THANKS, BABO! I LUUUUV YOUR COOKIES.
OC.CHIP OOKIES
MUNCH! MUNCH!
CHOC.CHIP COOKIES
CLINK!

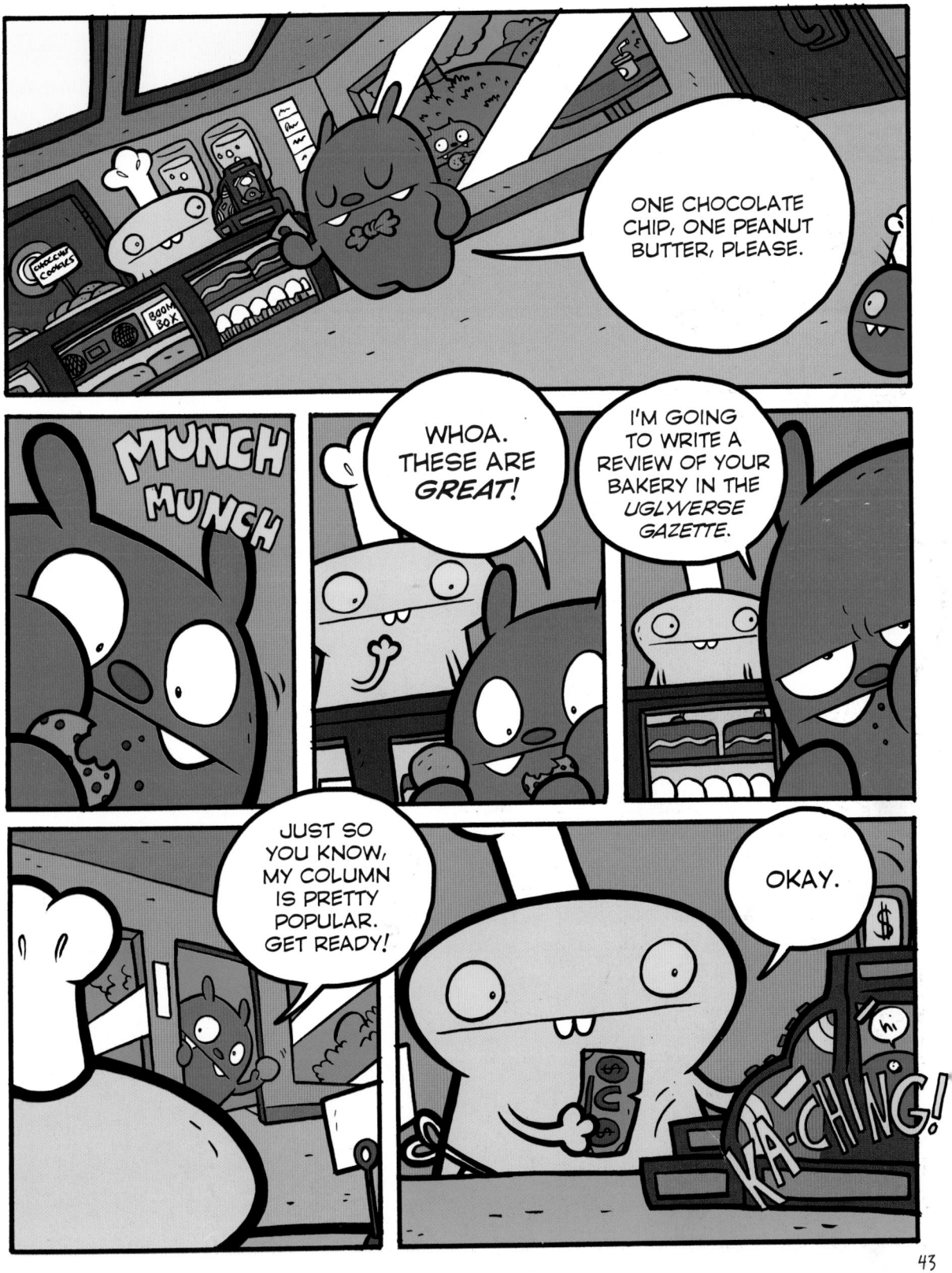
ONE CHOCOLATE CHIP, ONE PEANUT BUTTER, PLEASE.
CHOCOLATE COOKIES
BOOM BOX
MUNCH MUNCH
WHOA. THESE ARE GREAT!
I'M GOING TO WRITE A REVIEW OF YOUR BAKERY IN THE UGLYVERSE GAZETTE.
JUST SO YOU KNOW, MY COLUMN IS PRETTY POPULAR. GET READY!
OKAY.
KA-CHING!

THE NEXT DAY
BABO'S
BABO'S
ONE PEANUT BUTTER COOKIE, BAKERDUDE.
BOOM
OH NO, OH NO. IS HE OUT? ARE THEY SOLD OUT?
WHEW!
CLINK!
BOOM BOX

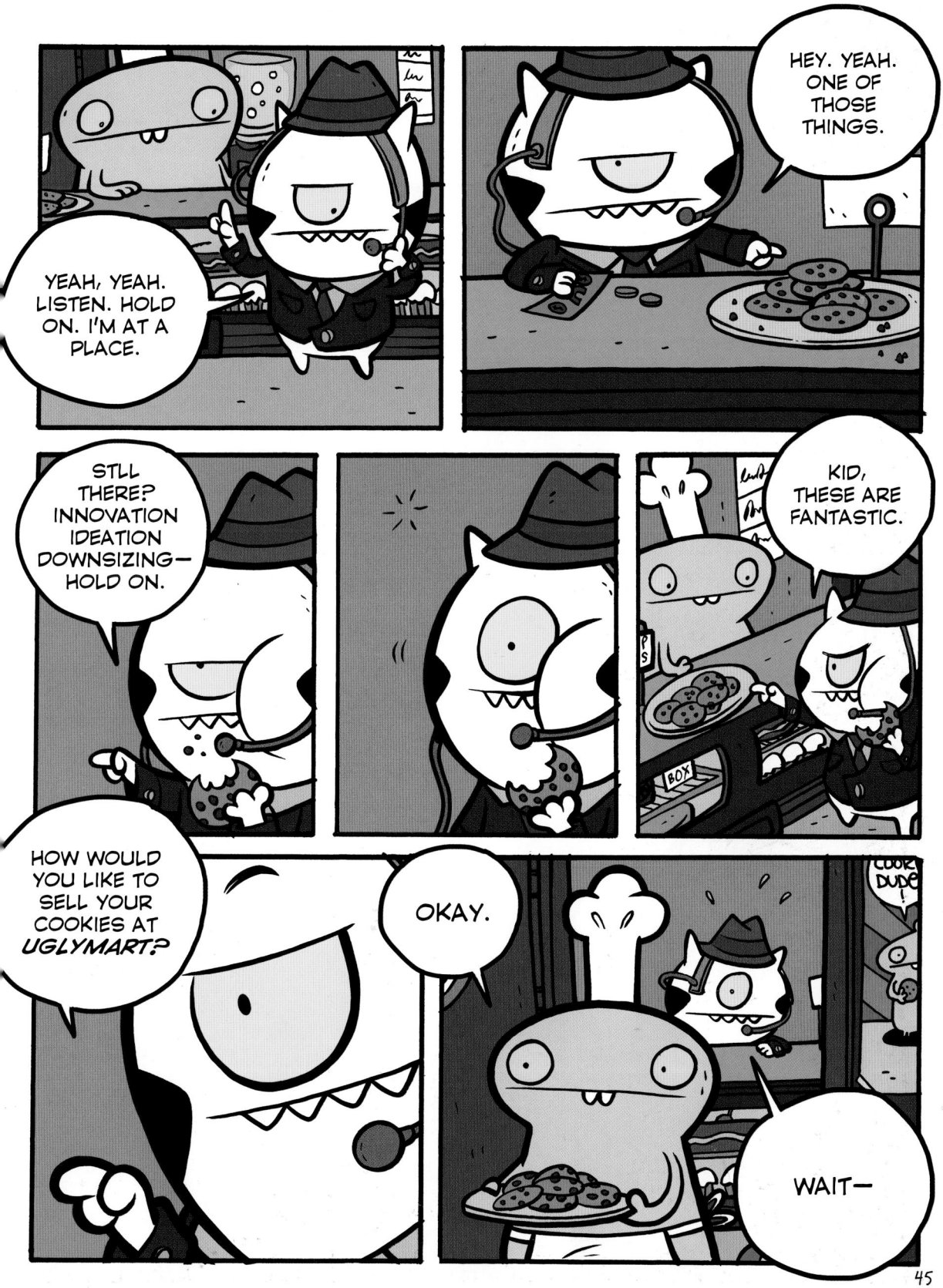
YEAH, YEAH. LISTEN. HOLD ON. I'M AT A PLACE.
HEY. YEAH. ONE OF THOSE THINGS.
STLL THERE? INNOVATION IDEATION DOWNSIZING— HOLD ON.
KID, THESE ARE FANTASTIC.
BOX
HOW WOULD YOU LIKE TO SELL YOUR COOKIES AT *UGLYMART?*
OKAY.
WAIT—

WE'LL NEED A HUGE KITCHEN! LOTS OF BAKERS! BOXES! LABELS! WITH ANY LUCK WE'LL BE UP-AND-RUNNING IN A FEW MONTHS!
FROSTBITE WUZ HERE
BABO'S
ROLL!
ROLL!
ROLL!
HAVE YOU SEEN ME?
I AM UGLY!
Beep!! Beep!
BABO'S CHOCOLATE CHIP
BABO'S ICED GINGERBREAD
BABO'S PEANUT BUTTER
CELERY
HMM... SIGN HERE.

SOON...
DESTROY
ALL OBSTACLES
Pop!
Live
UGLYMART
BABO! LISTEN. WE'RE GOING TO NEED TO QUADRUPLE OUR ORDER!
OKAY.
CHOC.CHIP COOKIES
AND A COUPLE MORE VARIETIES?
Live
BABO'S
OKAY.
HOW DOES HE DO IT?!
ADMINISTRATIVE ASSISTANT! BRING ME SOMETHING SHINY AND EXPENSIVE THAT I'LL GET BORED WITH ALMOST IMMEDIATELY!
BEEP!

ROUND FRUITS!
FOOD
PIZZA
CARROT
BABO'S
HEE HEE HEE! SHINY!
ZIP!
BABO'S
SIGH.
RRUHM!
BABO'S
BABO'S
VROOOM!

A DOZEN BLACK-AND-WHITE COOKIES.
NO! WE AGREED ON 12!
THERE HE IS!
EAT!
2765
DON'T EAT THE FLOUR
BABO! YOUR COOKIES ARE THE BEST EVER! THEY'RE THE HOTTEST THINGS ON THE *PLANET!*
2765
TELL US: HOW DO YOU DO IT?!
UGLY 2 TV
OKAY.
UGLY 2 TV
2765
THIS IS IT, FOLKS. THE SCOOP OF THE CENTURY!

BOX
GASP!

END
SQUAAAAWK!
SQUAAAAWK!
SQUAAAAWK!
SQUAAAAWK!
SQUAAAAWK!
SQUAAAAWK!
SQUAAAAWK!

Delicious
BY JOE LEDBETTER
YOU LOOK DELICIOUS.
NO, YOU LOOK DELICIOUS.
YOU'RE BOTH DELICIOUS.
CHOMP!!
HEY FIRE-CAT, DID YOU SEE MY LUNCH?
I DID! IT WAS DELICIOUS! WHATCHA GONNA DO ABOUT IT?
THAT'S THE LAST STRAW, FIRE-CAT! AN ICE-BAT CAN ONLY TAKE SO MUCH!
JLED

SWEET. THAT SHOULD HOLD HIM FOR A BIT. NOW, WHAT TO DO ABOUT LUNCH.
GRRRRR
FLWAPP!
SPACK
HELP
ME TOO!
mmmmmmm... DELICIOUS!
JED

SNAP
YAY!
UFF...
WHOOSH
THANKS, FIRE-CAT. YOU SAVED ME!
WHO ELSE AM I GOING TO STEAL MY LUNCH FROM? BESIDES, YOUR COOKING IS DELISH!
YOU KNOW, JUST 'CAUSE I'M AN ICE-BAT AND YOU'RE A FIRE-CAT DOESN'T MEAN WE CAN'T BE FRIENDS.
WHY DON'T WE JUST EAT LUNCH TOGETHER?
BUDDIES?
PALS!
UHH... SO WHO'S BUYING?
END!

MOVER & LITTLE BENT'S Lunch on the Goooooo
Are you like us? Always on the move, making it loathsome, nay, IMPOSSIBLE to stop for lunch?
Frankly, just standing here and talking is driving me NUTS.
So what do fidgety fellas and ladyfellas on the go do when midday hunger strikes?
WRAP IT UP!
Okay. I know. I'm trying to finish this as fast as possible.
No, I mean WRAP IT UP. The food. We talked about this.
GLASS
CANS
TRAVIS NICHOLS '13

Oh yeah. WRAP. As in lunch wraps.

Right. So tell them what they need.

Hold on. I'm at the bottom of the ocean studying seaweed.

Okay. I'm back. They need food. And wraps.

Yeah yeah. Then put the food in the wrap and go.

OKAYBYE

DON'T OVER DO IT!
WE'LL BRING THIS MUCH TO THE PASTRY CONVENTION AND THAT'S IT.
OK.
NOT SPENDING A PENNY OVER WHAT'S IN MY HAND.
DUDE...
THIS YEAR IT'S HUGE
X 100
X 100
X 100
ALWAYS THE LONGEST LINE AT THE SHOW.
YEAH.
YEAH.
ATM
SUSAN DAVID

HOT IN THE MADE
BLAAAA AAAAAAA AAAH...
KNOW WHAT WOULD BE AWESOME?
YEAAAAAAAAH
LEMONADE!

SUGAR!
SUGAR

WATER!

LEMONS!

LET'S DO THIS.

IT'S NOT... RIGHT.

MORE SUGAR?

NO, THAT'S NOT IT... Sure is hot out here...
MORE LEMONS?
HMM... NOPE. MORE WATER?
NOW IT'S...NOT SWEET ENOUGH? I DON'T KNOW.
POUR

TOO SWEET!
SUGAR!
TOO SOUR!
PAF
HERE. LET'S USE THIS.
THAT'S NOT IT!
WISH WE COULD FIGURE THIS OUT!
I REALLY... JUST... DON'T...

WHEW! SURE IS HOT! OOH! LEMONADE?

NEEDS MORE LEMONS.

SEE, THAT'S WHAT I THOUGHT, BUT I DON'T KNOW.

OKAY, DRAG IT OVER HERE!

THIS SHOULD DO IT!
I HOPE SO! I'M MELTING!

MORE... LEMONS?
HEY EVERYBODY!
WHAT'S GOING ON?
THAT'S IT!
FINALLY!
END

SWEET VICTORY
CUPPA
HEY, JEERO! WANT A BITE OF MY PANCAKES? THEY'RE SOOO GOOOOOOD.
YAAAAAAAA
TRAY: BREAKFAST 2MORROW?
TKA TKA TKA
JEERO: WHAT WOULD WE BE HAVING?
"THE USUAL. HASH-BROWNS, PANC—"
FWIP

LATER...
UM... THIS DOESN'T LOOK LIKE MUCH OF A PIZZA PARTY.
WAGE IS GETTING THE PIZZA. WE'RE HERE MOSTLY FOR YOU.
YEAH. WHAT'S UP WITH THIS PANCAKE THING?
WHAT'S GOING ON, BUDDY?
I CAN'T... IT'S TOO PAINFUL.
IT'S OKAY, JEERO. WE'RE YOUR PALS. YOU CAN TELL US ANYTHING.

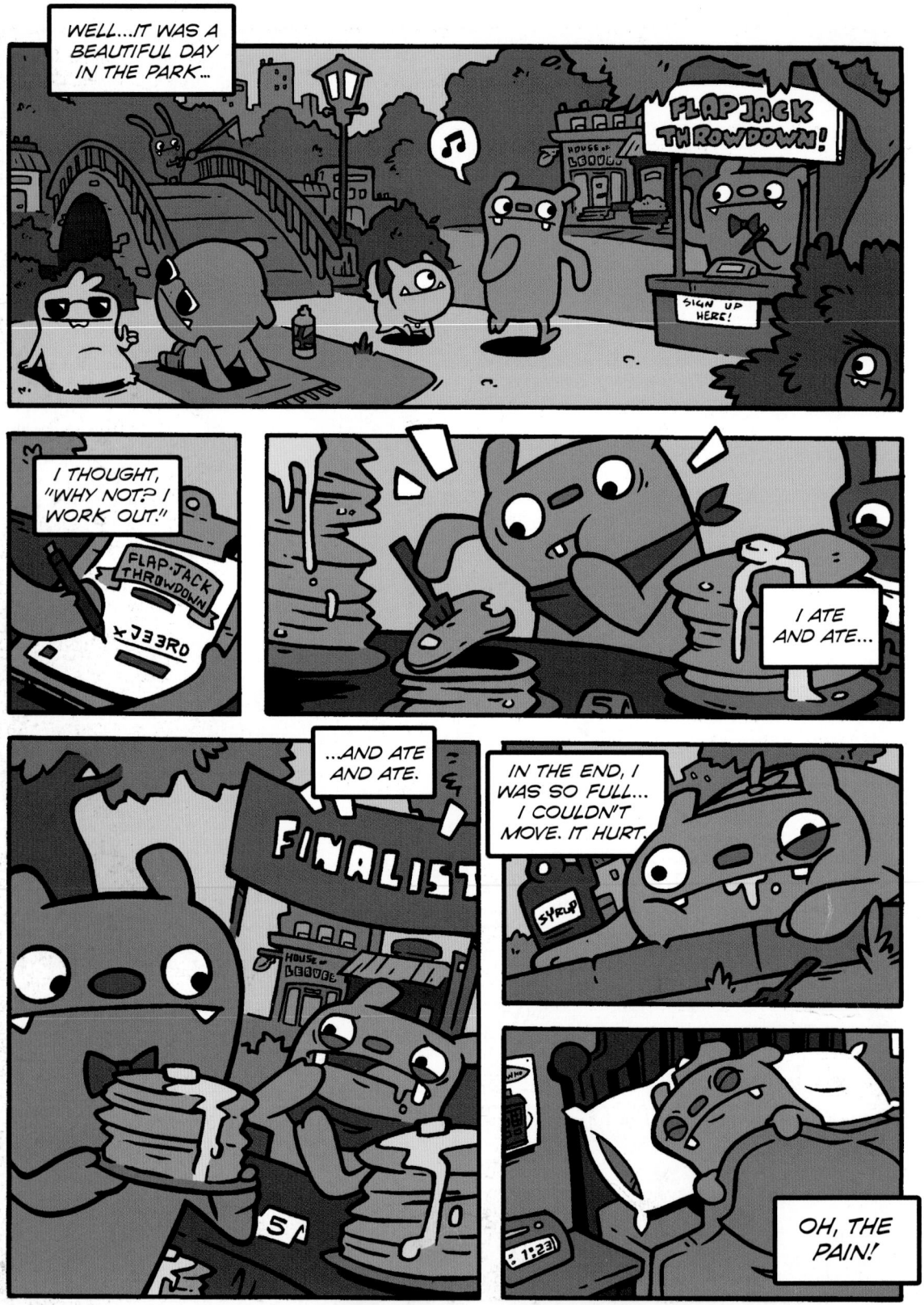
WELL...IT WAS A BEAUTIFUL DAY IN THE PARK...
FLAPJACK THROWDOWN!
HOUSE OF LEGUME
SIGN UP HERE!
I THOUGHT, "WHY NOT? I WORK OUT."
FLAP·JACK THROWDOWN
I ATE AND ATE...
...AND ATE AND ATE.
FINALIST
HOUSE OF LEGUME
IN THE END, I WAS SO FULL... I COULDN'T MOVE. IT HURT.
SYRUP
OH, THE PAIN!

WAIT. THAT WAS THURSDAY.
YEAH. I GOT SECOND PLACE.
I would've won if the pancakes had been blueberry.
WELL... I JUST... NEVER AGAIN.
HEY, ALL! I GOT KICKED OUT OF THE PIZZA PLACE, SO I GOT WAFFLES.
GO-GO WAFFLES!!
YUM!!
GO-GO WAFFLES!
END!

TRAGER NICHOLS

UGSN
BLACK BELT JUICE NINJA NATOR
Ψ29.99
500/500
0:28:52
Simply load the Chamber of Ultimate Vigor.
UGSN
BLACK BELT JUICE NINJA NATOR
Ψ29.99
500/500
0:28:47
Folks, this included recipe is full of vitamin-rich vegetables, whole grains...
UGSN
BLACK BELT JUICE NINJA NATOR
Ψ29.99
500/500
0:28:44
...quasi-legal nutrient powder blends...
UGSN
BLACK BELT JUICE NINJA NATOR
Ψ29.99
500/500
0:28:40
And pineapple for a little extra sweetness!
UGSN
BLACK BELT JUICE NINJA NATOR
Ψ29.99
500/500
0:28:32
Now, the patent-pending Ninjatronic 22-blade system in the Ninjanator can Blenderize™ ANYTHING.
BBJN
TM
UGSN
BLACK BELT JUICE NINJA NATOR
Ψ29.99
500/500
0:28:23
FOLKS, THE NINJANATOR IS NOW LIQUIDINATING™ THESE INGREDIENTS BETTER THAN ANY BLENDER IN THE HISTORY OF HOME APPLIANCES!!!
RRRRRR

UGSN
BLACK BELT JUICE NINJA NATOR
₩29.99
498/500
0:28:14
Ninja Batty Shogun will now show you how this simple, delicious, three-gallon juice can give your body an entire week's worth of nutrition.
RRP!

UGSN
BLACK BELT JUICE NINJA NATOR
₩29.99
498/500
0:28:08

UGSN
BLACK BELT JUICE NINJA NATOR
₩29.99
498/500
0:28:01
DOWN THE HATCH!

UGSN
BLACK BELT JUICE NINJA NATOR
₩29.99
498/500
0:27:53
Mmmmmmfffggrrr!!!!

UGSN
BLACK BELT JUICE NINJA NATOR
₩29.99
498/500
0:27:49
G-g-g-gulp!

UGSN
BLACK BELT JUICE NINJA NATOR
₩29.99
498/500
0:27:45
Ooh... This is bad.

UGSN
BLACK BELT JUICE NINJA NATOR
$29.99
498/500
0:27:43
OUTTATHEWAY!
UGSN
BLACK BELT JUICE NINJA NATOR
$29.99
498/500
0:27:42
CRASH!
THE CAMERA! WATCH OUT!
UGSN
BLACK BELT JUICE NINJA NATOR
$29.99
498/500
0:27:38
BLEEEAGH! BLARG! FFFFT!
UGSN
BLACK BELT JUICE NINJA NATOR
$29.99
498/500
0:27:35
CAMERA Two! CAMERA Two!
UUUUGGG....
UGSN
BLACK BELT JUICE NINJA NATOR
$29.99
114/500
0:27:31
Folks, let me assure you that this product –
UGSN
BLACK BELT JUICE NINJA NATOR
$29.99
SOLD OUT!
0:27:29
Oh. We... we sold out. Wow. Thanks for watching.

and so...
UGSN
OBLITERINATOR
Hi, folks! Jeero and Big Toe here with the must-have gadget for every home.
LITERIZ-NATOR
Ψ39.99
498/498
0:30:00
UGSN
OBLITERINATOR
What if I told you that this one item could eliminate every problem in your LIFE?
Ψ39.99
498/498
0:29:51
UGSN
OBLITERINATOR
Bad grade on a book report?
JEERO G-
"A tale of Two UGLIES"
It was the best of... Thither...
Ψ39.99
498/498
0:29:46
UGSN
OBLITERINATOR
Mountain of dirty dishes in the sink?
Ψ39.99
498/498
0:29:44
UGSN
OBLITERINATOR
Rusted-out car in the driveway?
Ψ39.99
497/498
0:29:41
UGSN
OBLITERINATOR
OBLITERIZINATE IT!
Ψ39.99
497/498
0:29:38
END!

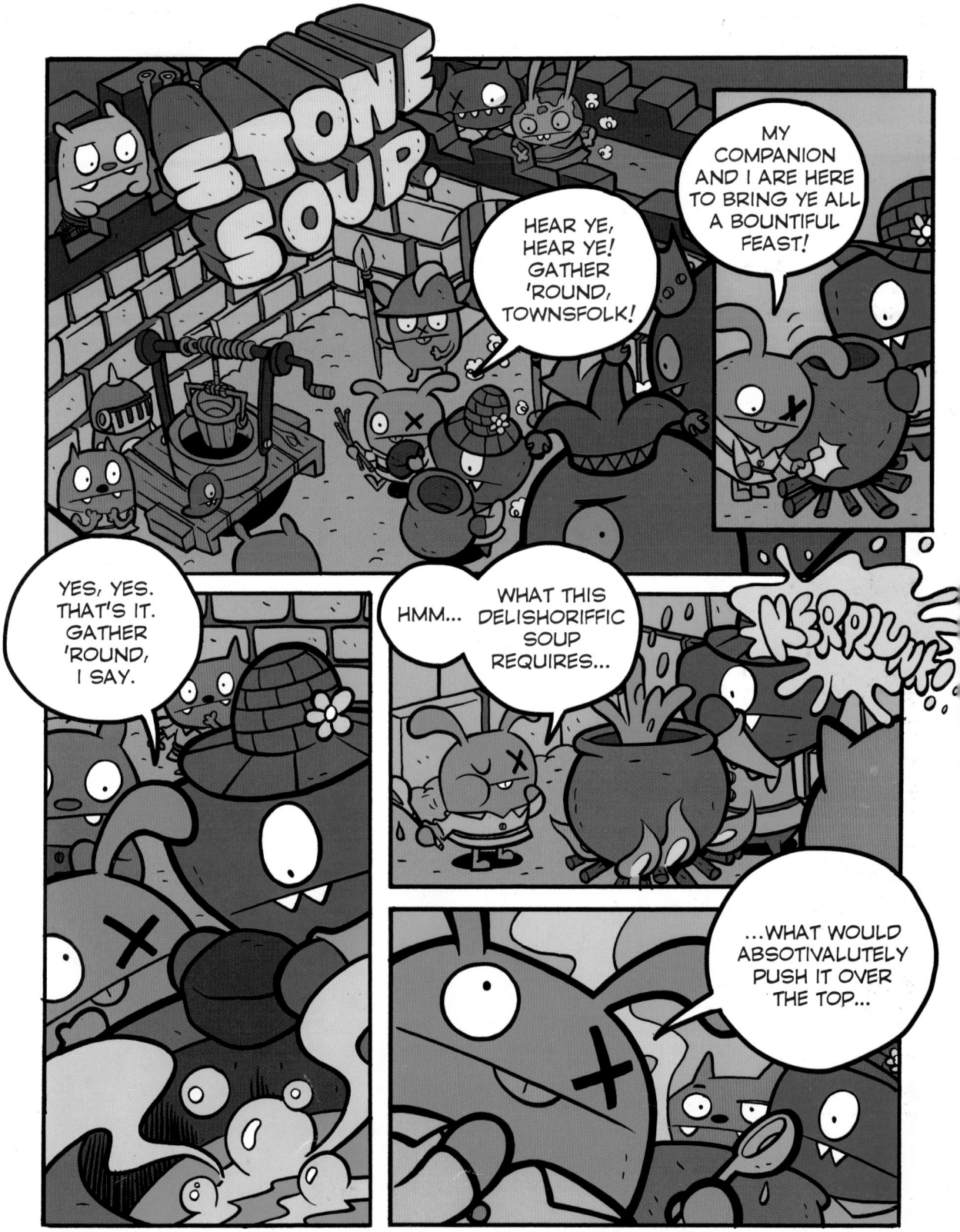
STONE SOUP
HEAR YE, HEAR YE! GATHER 'ROUND, TOWNSFOLK!
MY COMPANION AND I ARE HERE TO BRING YE ALL A BOUNTIFUL FEAST!
YES, YES. THAT'S IT. GATHER 'ROUND, I SAY.
HMM...
WHAT THIS DELISHORIFFIC SOUP REQUIRES...
KERPLUNK!
...WHAT WOULD ABSOTIVALUTELY PUSH IT OVER THE TOP...

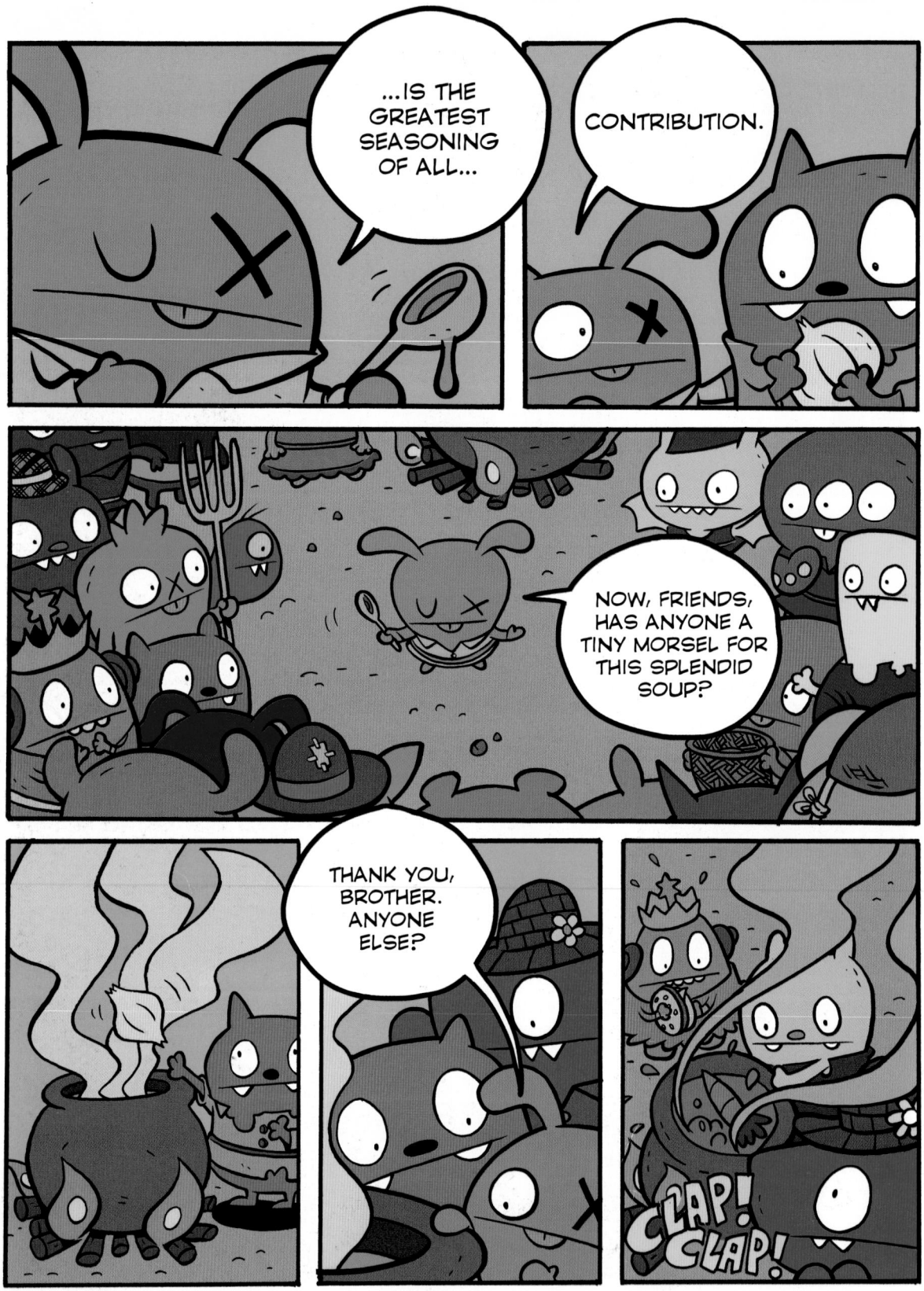
...IS THE GREATEST SEASONING OF ALL...
CONTRIBUTION.
NOW, FRIENDS, HAS ANYONE A TINY MORSEL FOR THIS SPLENDID SOUP?
THANK YOU, BROTHER. ANYONE ELSE?
CLAP! CLAP!

POP!
WOW

PROTEIN POWDA
I'M BUFF

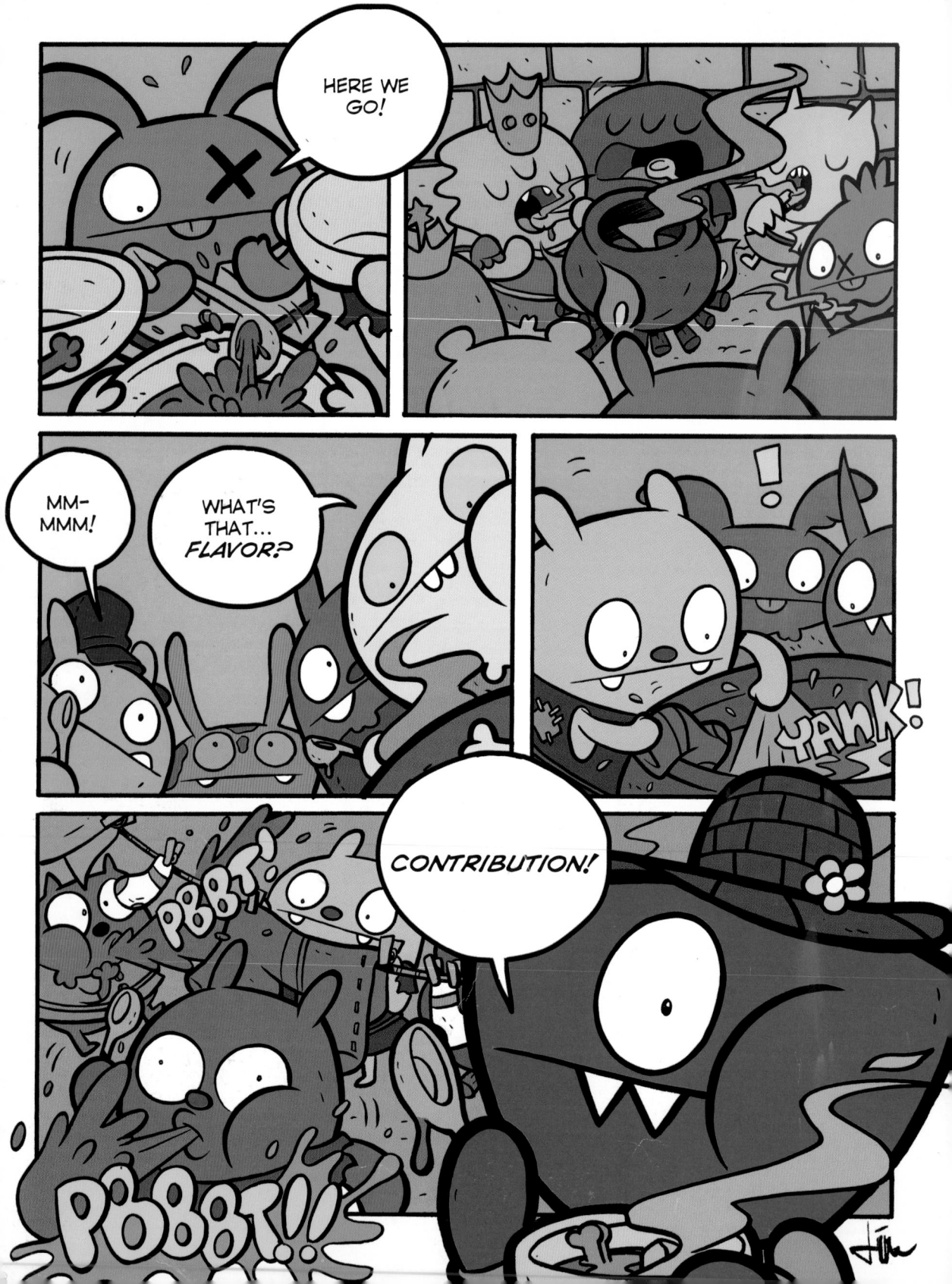
HERE WE GO!
MM-MMM!
WHAT'S THAT... FLAVOR?
!
YANK!
CONTRIBUTION!
PBBT!
PBBBT!!

BACK IN THE UGLY DAY

BROUGHT

SUN-MIN KIM & DAVID HORVATH

are best known for creating the world of Uglydoll, which started as a line of handmade plush dolls and has since grown into a brand loved by all ages around the world. Their works can be found everywhere from the Moma in Tokyo and the Louvre in Paris, to the windows of their very own Uglydoll shop in Seoul. Sun-Min and David's very first conversation was about the meaning of "ugly." To them, ugly means unique and different, that which makes us who we are. It should never be hidden, but shouted from the rooftops! They wanted to build a world that showed the twists and turns that make us who we are, inside and out, because the whole world benefits when we embrace our true, twisty-turny selves. So, ugly is the new beauty. This Uglydoll comic features some of Sun-Min and David's heroes from the pop art and comic art world.

TRAVIS NICHOLS

is the author and illustrator of several books for kids and post-kids, including *The Monster Doodle Book*, *Punk Rock Etiquette* and *Matthew Meets the Man*. He previously drew comics for the late, great *Nickelodeon Magazine*. His deepest, most secret wish is to wake up as a gnome and spend his days building wooden locks, eating tiny biscuits and hanging out with birds. He can be found eating watermelon over the sink or online.

IAN MCGINTY

is a real smiley dude! And he wants to know where you got that cool lunchbox! You know, the one with the dinosaur riding a great white shark?
Oh, is this Gilbert Johnson? No? Gosh, sorry for bothering you! Um...okay, bye.

TO YOU BY:

PHILLIP JACOBSON

is a graduate of the Savannah College of Art and Design sequential art program. His earlier works include the self-published titles *Battle Mammals* and *Pancakes for Yeti*. Some of his influences include Bryan Lee O'Malley, Madeline Rupert and Craig Bartlett. He would like to thank his late grandmother Mary Ann Hill for constantly encouraging him to draw when he was little and for inspiring him to pursue his artistic goals.

DAVE COOPER

is a comic book guy, a gallery painting guy, a kid's book guy, and an aspiring television guy. He likes making up stuff, doesn't really matter what for.

JOE LEDBETTER'S

distinctive style is deeply influenced by classic animation, underground comics, skateboarding and 1980s' video games. Over the years, Ledbetter has created an incredible cast of creatures to personify the human condition. With crisp bold lines and a vibrant palette, he mixes irony, social criticism and mischief, making his work universal and unmistakable.
Ledbetter is best known for his innovative and distinctive designer toys.

MICHAEL E. WIGGAM

is a professional comic book colorist whose work includes *Voltron Force* for VIZ Media, *Star Wars: Clone Wars* for Dark Horse Comics, Raymond E. Feist's *Magician Master: Enter the Great One* for Marvel Comics, *R.P.M.* and *I.C.E.* for 12 Gauge Comics, and various other publications. He was born and raised in Florida but has lived in Europe and seven U.S. states. Currently, he is earning an MFA from Savannah College of Art and Design.

3 1901 05315 3328